# Frankie's Halloween
## A PKU Friendly Holiday

Written and Illustrated by Kacie Foos

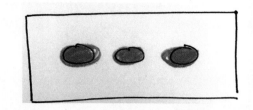

## INTRODUCTION:

Phenylketonuria, also known as PKU, is a Genetic Metabolic Disease in which the body cannot break down an amino acid called Phenylalanine, which is found mostly in foods that contain protein.

There is no cure. This book series is to spread awareness, and open a conversation to this and other metabolic diseases.

The world is full of unique and extraordinary people. Our hope is that these books will open your mind, and your hearts, for families with dietary requests.

And that a day may come that all of these requests will be met without judgment, but rather kindness and compassion.

# Frankie's Halloween
# A PKU Friendly Holiday
## Written and Illustrated by Kacie Foos
## Recipe Created by Tony Spatafora

For more on what's the Dish with Tony Spatafora subscribe to his
YouTube Channel http://www.youtube.com/user/DishitOutTV
or follow on Twitter @GetDish

Fall is here! The leaves are piling on the ground, there is a cold breeze in the air, and pumpkins have arrived! That's right, its HALLOWEEN!
These are some of Frankie's favorite things to do with her Family on Halloween.

Frankie and her parents are starting their Halloween adventure at their local Pumpkin Patch. Frankie and her parents go every year.

Frankie loved the corn maze. It was so much fun. They kept getting lost in the maze but it was quite an adventure.

# Can you find your way through the Corn Maze?
## Beware of Monsters!

After the maze Frankie and her parents enjoyed her favorite Fall treat, a candied apple.

Frankie was so excited to carve her pumpkin when she got home. Her Dad helped her cut the top off so she could scoop out all the inside.

After Frankie finished her Halloween Pumpkin she needed to take her weekly blood test.
Her Dad made her laugh when he surprised her dressed as a vampire.

# Time to Change into our Halloween Costumes!
## Frankie is a Pumpkin Princess!

Frankie loved "Trick or Treating" with her Mom and Dad.

Frankie loves all of the decorations, the fun costumes, and running up to the door to say, "Trick or Treat!"

After a long fun day, it's time for dinner. Mom is serving a yummy low protein Pumpkin Soup for dinner. This is one of Frankie's favorite Fall meals.

After a warm bowl of pumpkin soup Frankie and her parents got ready for a Halloween Movie, complete with Popcorn for Mom and Dad and PKU friendly candy for Frankie. What a wonderful way to end the perfect Halloween!

# The End

Happy 2nd Halloween our darling girl! We look forward to celebrating with you through the years to come.

# A PKU FRIENDLY HALLOWEEN CANDY LIST

| | |
|---|---|
| Airheads | Bottlecaps |
| Candy Necklaces | Dots |
| Fruit Runt | Fun Dip |
| Gobstoppers | Jolly Ranchers |
| Laffy Taffy | Lifesavers |
| Mike & Ike | Nerds |
| Pez | Pixy Stix |
| Ring Pops | Salt Water Taffy |
| Smarties | Sour Patch |
| Sour Punch Candy | Suckers |
| Lolly Pops | Dum Dums |
| Swedish Fish | SweeTARTS |

# Frankie's PKU Friendly Halloween Pumpkin Soup

## Recipe Created by Tony Spatafora

## Ingredients

2 cups mashed roasted pumpkin
1/4 cup think sliced leeks
1/2 cup chopped celery
1 cup chopped carrots
2 tablespoons margarine
2 cups vegetable stock
2 cups apple cider
1 bay leaf
1 teaspoon allspice
1 teaspoon cinnamon
1/2 teaspoon cardamom
salt and pepper to taste

Toss cubed pumpkin in vegetable oil, salt and pepper. Roast at 400 degrees until golden, about 30-45 minutes. Let cool.

Melt margarine over medium- high heat in soup pot. Add leeks, carrots, celery, and bay leaf. Saute until tender.

Add stock and cider and bring to medium boil. Add Pumpkin and stir.

Working in batches, puree soup using food processor until smooth. Make sure to remove bay leaf before processing.

Return soup to pot and add spices. Adjust seasonings to taste. If thicker soup desired add 1 teaspoon cornstarch to cold water to make a slurry. Add slurry to boiling soup, stirring often, for one minute. Garish with flash fried leeks. Serve and enjoy! Yummy!

CPSIA information can be obtained at www.ICGtesting.com
Printed in the USA
BVIW12n0857210818
525124BV00019B/262